MACY AND THE
KING'S TOURNAMENT

WRITTEN BY REBECCA L. SCHMIDT

SCHOLASTIC INC.

Published by Scholastic Inc., *Publishers since 1920*. SCHOLASTIC and associated logos are trademarks and/or registered trademarks of Scholastic Inc.

ISBN: 978-1-338-05558-0

10 9 8 7 6 5 4 3 2 1   17 18 19 20 21

Printed in the U.S.A.   40

First printing 2017

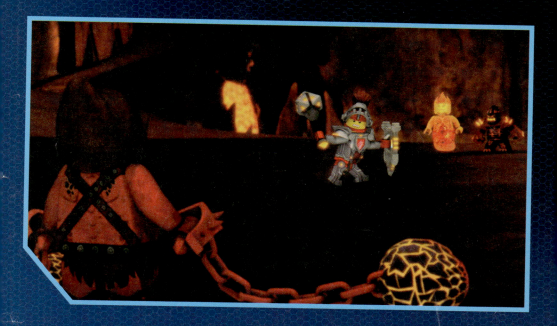

Macy at Work

Deep in the dark woods, Macy, a member of the NEXO KNIGHTS team, was hard at work. Surrounded by some of Jestro's toughest minions, she didn't have any backup. She had to face Beast Master, Flama, and Moltor on her own.

Beast Master wrapped his ball and chain around the knight. She was caught! But Macy was too tough to give up. She used Beast Master's own weapons against him and pulled the monster down flat on his face. Next, she turned to face Flama and Moltor.

Suddenly, Flama and Moltor didn't seem quite as scary. They were wearing princess dresses! What magic was this?

"Macy, which dress would you like to wear for your father's birthday party?" asked a voice from nowhere.

Macy recognized that voice. "Mom! What are you doing here?"

The dark woods, lava, and monsters all disappeared. Macy had been in the training room the entire time!

"Your mace work makes your momma proud," Queen Halbert said as she entered the room. "But I'm afraid your father still thinks of you as his 'little princess.' It would so please your father to see you in a nice dress at his party, Macy."

Macy wished her father would understand that she was a knight first, and a princess second. But she also didn't want to disappoint her dad on his birthday.

"Okay . . . As long as it's a small party . . . where no one has to see me in a girly gown," Macy said.

The King's Birthday Feast

"**W**elcome, citizens of Knightonia, to the biggest birthday celebration of the year!" Herb Herbertson announced. The king's birthday party had turned out to be anything but small.

The Joustdome was packed. And right at the center of it was Macy—in a sparkly princess gown. She was eating dinner with her parents, as everyone in the entire kingdom watched her.

Macy wasn't the only one upset at the dinner. A guest at the party, Jorah Tightwad, didn't like all the attention the king and his knights were getting.

"Ha! Those knights are next to nothing compared to my Tighty Knighties," Jorah bragged. "After all," he asked the king, "how many magical books have your NEXO KNIGHTS heroes recovered?"

Macy and the other knights gasped as Jorah pulled out the magical Book of Envy!

Macy Makes a Bet

"**O**h! I guess those Tighty Knighties really ARE amazing," King Halbert said.

Macy knew she had to prove that the NEXO KNIGHTS heroes were the best. The queen suggested they settle the argument the next day, at the king's birthday celebration tournament. The NEXO KNIGHTS heroes versus the Tighty Knighties to see which team was the best

Jorah wanted a prize once his knights won the tournament. A kiss! Macy said yes, but only if Jorah would kiss "Lance's sweetheart" if the NEXO KNIGHTS team won. Jorah agreed.

Macy laughed. Jorah had no idea that he had just agreed to kiss Lance's pet pig!

An Evil Plan

Meanwhile, Jestro and The Book of Monsters were planning the next step in their scheme to conquer the kingdom.

Jestro cast a magic spell to show them their next evil book. Soon, the spell showed them a vision of the king's birthday dinner. There was Jorah Tightwad holding The Book of Envy— exactly what Jestro and The Book of Monsters were looking for!

Macy Sidelined

The next day was the king's tournament. The crowd roared as the knights were announced—all the knights except for Macy. It was still the king's birthday celebration, so Macy was stuck on the sidelines in her sparkly dress.

Herb Herbertson announced the Tighty Knighties. "Say hello to Jousting Beeber, Brickney Spears, Shia LaBlade, and The Blok!"

The crowd roared. The Tighty Knighties were a hit!

"You've *got* to be kidding me," Clay said.

"Come on! This'll be a cinch! We've got awesome-sauce-attitude!" Aaron told the other knights.

"Way more experience," Clay agreed.

"A fuller stomach," Axl said. With all this on their side, how could the knights lose?

The King's Tournament

Clay was first up against Shia LaBlade. The challenge was to carve a sculpture out of a single block of wood. Clay confidently used his sword to make stick figures. He looked proudly at LaBlade—until all Clay's figures toppled over.

LaBlade attacked his own piece of wood and crafted a heroic sculpture of Jorah Tightwad.

"Whoa! Any way you slice it, the Tighty Knighties have taken the lead!" Herb Herbertson announced.

Next up, Lance and Jousting Beeber were ready to face off—as soon as they were done greeting their adoring fans.

Lance was used to getting all the attention, but the crowd *loved* Jousting Beeber. Lance's side of the stadium was empty. "Got to kick this up a notch," Lance said.

Lance rode his hover horse across the stadium, trying to win back his fans. But instead of cheers, he heard a fan scream, "We love you, Beeber!"

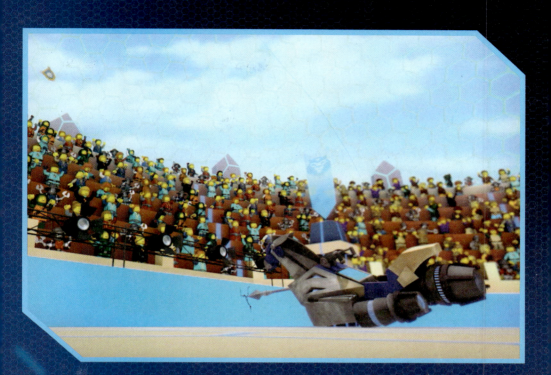

Lance turned to see what was happening, but because he wasn't paying attention his hover horse slammed right into the side of the arena. Lance went flying!

"Ooh! Beeber knocked Lance off his horse without a joust—now *that's* class!" Alice Squires said.

Macy hoped that Aaron could get the knights back on track as he battled Brickney Spears. But it did not go well.

Aaron took down ten bull's-eyes with ten arrows, but Brickney used her one fancy spear to take down ten bull's-eyes! She had won!

"One more event," Alice Squires announced. "But we might as well call it now: The NEXO KNIGHTS heroes are the EXO-knights."

"C'mon, Alice, I'm sure Axl won't let his team be shut out. Let's watch him as he takes on The Blok in . . . Bowling for Bots!"

The challenge was to knock over as many Squirebots as the knights could with giant boulders. After the first round, Axl and The Blok were tied one to one.

"This should be quite the contest. So grab a snack, sit back, and watch 'em roll!" Alice Squires said. But that was exactly the wrong thing to say.

"'Snack? Roll? Mm . . . " Axl said as he looked into the stands. He was a little hungry. He hit his next boulder halfheartedly and ran to get a bite to eat. Instead of hitting the Squirebots, the boulder just rolled right past them. The Blok slammed his boulder so hard that it broke into tiny pieces that hit every single Squirebot—including Axl's!

"Oh! Looks like Axl chose vittles over victory!" Herb Herbertson said.

General Magmar's Siege Tower

Macy couldn't believe it. The knights had lost! Suddenly, there was a loud *boom*! Macy gasped as the wall of the Joustdome exploded and Jestro and his horde of monsters entered the stadium. Leading the charge was General Magmar and his Siege Tower. The tower launched fiery blasts into the stadium as the Tighty Knighties and NEXO KNIGHTS heroes ran for cover.

"Grab the book from Lord Tightyness there!" The Book of Monsters ordered.

Jorah Tightwad clutched The Book of Envy closer. "No, it's mine! Tighty Knighties! Defend me!" he ordered.

But the Tighty Knighties were too scared to take on Jestro's army of monsters.

"Us?" Shia LaBlade gulped.

"But . . . those are *real* bad guys!" The Blok
said.

"With *real* weapons!" Brickney Spears said.
She fumbled with her fancy spear, but it came
apart in her hands. It may have been nice for
tricks, but Brickney wasn't prepared for real
battle.

But at least Brickney was trying. Jousting Beeber was running around the stadium
screaming. He wasn't going to be any help
defeating the bad guys.

Shia LaBlade drew his sword and spun it fancily in the air. But he wasn't carving wood anymore; he was fighting real bad guys! The monsters easily knocked him aside.

There were too many Globlins for The Blok. They dragged him to the ground and out of the stadium. The Tighty Knighties were defeated!

Jorah and The Book of Envy

Macy cornered Jorah. "There's no way your knights beat Jestro's monsters in a battle over that book!"

"Perhaps I exaggerated a teensy tiny bit?" Jorah said. He admitted that the night of Merlok's battle at King Halbert's castle, he and his knights had been in the countryside. In the magical explosion, books had been flung everywhere. The Book of Envy had landed right at his feet! The Tighty Knighties hadn't had to fight anyone for it.

Jorah was so busy telling his story that he didn't notice Jestro taking The Book of Envy right out of his hands!

"We have the book! Now . . . how about some light entertainment?" Jestro said. He missed performing for the kingdom each year on the king's birthday.

"No! Just destroy it all! Starting with the pretty little princess here," The Book of Monsters said.

NEXO Powers!

That was the last straw. "One thing about this dress: It's really good for hiding my mace and shield," Macy said, as she pulled out her weapons seemingly from midair.

"Merlok! NEXOOO KNIGHTS!"

"Nexo Power: Majesty of Benevolence!" Merlok 2.0 cried from the NEXO KNIGHTS team's Fortrex.

Macy's dress disappeared and was replaced with her armor. She began to climb Magmar's Siege Tower.

"I shall not just destroy you!" the general said. "I shall obliterate! Devastate!"

Macy sprung over the side of the tower. "Don't worry: I'm fine just simply defeating you!" she cried. As Magmar charged, Macy swung her mace at his legs, knocking him down. Macy hit a switch and the Siege Tower transformed into vehicle mode, throwing Magmar down to the arena.

The other knights had all downloaded their NEXO Powers and were proving why they were heroes. Clay whacked Whiparella and General Magmar with his mighty sword. Lance scooped Beast Master up with his lance and flung him across the arena.

Aaron fired from his crossbow, dissolving Whiparella. Axl took out a mass of Scurriers and Globlins with his mighty ax. They may not have beaten the Tighty Knighties at tricks, but the knights were fantastic at taking down the bad guys.

Macy Victorious

The monsters retreated. Macy and the knights had saved the day again!

"We have our winners!" the king declared as he held up the arms of the knights.

The Tighty Knighties were good at tournaments and shows. But when it came to protecting the kingdom, no one could beat the NEXO KNIGHTS heroes.

All that was left was for Jorah to kiss Lance's sweetheart.

Jorah closed his eyes and puckered up and kissed . . .

A pig?!

"What!? That's her?!" Jorah said, disgusted.

The knights laughed: "Yep. Lance always calls his pet pig, 'sweetheart,'" Clay said.

"No . . . No . . . NOOOO!" Tightwad cried, fleeing in panic.

"This has been my BEST birthday celebration ever! But I need to have a word with my daughter," King Halbert said.

Macy sighed. "I know what you're going to say, Dad. I'm a princess, and I need to act like one."

"This is true, but you are also an amazing knight!" the king said proudly.

Macy couldn't believe what she was hearing. Her father was proud of her?

"It's fine if you want to play princess, my dear. But what this kingdom really needs . . . what I really need . . . are great knights. And that's what you are, Macy . . . a great knight!"

This was all that Macy had ever desired. She wanted her father to be proud of her and the life she had chosen.

Now that she had her father's approval, it was time for Macy to get back to work—being a knight!

5